ANIMAL
RESCUE CENTER

The
Lost
Duckling

ANIMAL MAGIC

Other titles in the series:

ANIMAL
+ RESCUE CENTER

The Lost Duckling

by TINA NOLAN

tiger tales

This series is for my riding friend Shelley,
who cares about all animals.

tiger tales

5 River Road, Suite 128, Wilton, CT 06897
Published in the United States 2017
Originally published in Great Britain 2007
by the Little Tiger Group
Text copyright © 2007, 2017 Jenny Oldfield
Interior illustrations copyright © 2017 Artful Doodlers
Cover illustration copyright © 2017 Anna Chernyshova
Images courtesy of www.shutterstock.com
ISBN-13: 978-1-68010-406-6
ISBN-10: 1-68010-406-3
Printed in China
STP/1800/0130/0317

For more insight and activities, visit us at www.tigertalesbooks.com

Contents

ANIMAL MAGIC
RESCUE CENTER

🏠 HOME

💗 ADOPT

✋ FRIENDS

MEET THE ANIMALS IN NEED OF A HOME!

CLEO

A brown and white springer spaniel, 12 months old. Great with children. Loves long walks and swimming!

HUGO

A friendly, neutered brown rabbit. Litter-trained and likes to cuddle. Can you give him a home?

ROSIE

Good things come in small packages! A great child's pony with a calm temperament and beautiful brown eyes!

SITE SEARCH

NEWS

HELP US

CONTACT

DONATE!

PENNY

An older lady and an absolute sweetheart. This yellow Labrador will do anything for you. Can you give her a loving home?

CHARLIE

Okay, so he's loud! But Charlie wouldn't hurt a fly. A nosy, lovable donkey in need of a big field and caring owners.

BLOSSOM

A beautiful feline found wandering in the wild. Lots of TLC needed to turn Blossom into the ideal pet.

Chapter One

A Celebration

"'Spring into Action!'—I've always liked that," Mark Harrison said. "It's a great slogan for Animal Magic. 'Spring into Action!'—it sounds very positive."

"Thanks," Caleb said, staring longingly at his pizza.

The Harrisons—Mark, Heidi, Caleb, and Ella, plus Joel, Animal Magic's veterinary assistant—were celebrating at the best Italian restaurant in town.

"Hey, Caleb!" Ella objected. "I helped

you think of it, remember!"

"Spring into Action"—the springtime slogan for the rescue center—had worked wonders, and it was partly due to Ella and her brother Caleb working on the website together.

And right now the family had another reason to celebrate. "This is the time to look forward," Mom reminded them.

Dad nodded. "Absolutely! The Council finally said no to Mrs. Brooks's petition to have us closed down."

"That's worth celebrating!" Joel said.

"And look at how well we've been doing recently," Mom added. "Since early May we've found good homes for 18 out of the 20 dogs we've rescued, 12 out of 15 cats, 6 out of 6 hamsters, besides all the other small animals that have been brought in—rabbits, ferrets, mice—you name it, we've found a new home for it!"

"We're on a roll," Dad agreed. "I think the spring campaign is really working."

"Yes, it sure is!" Mom said, raising her glass. "Let's eat!"

Ella and Caleb didn't need to be told twice. They dove into their pizzas and chomped quietly.

"Ah, peace!" Dad joked. "I have found, over the years, that food is the only thing that keeps you two quiet."

Chewy, crusty pizza with slurpy tomato sauce, pepperoni, and melted cheese on top—yum! Ella munched in silence.

"Which gives me the chance to say thanks to everyone for all the effort you put in to keeping Animal Magic open," Mom went on. "It's been a stressful time, waiting for the Council to consider Mrs. Brooks's petition, but you all worked your socks off to make sure we got the right decision."

Joel, Ella, and Caleb grinned and nodded.

"Finally!" Caleb mumbled between mouthfuls.

"We won. Nothing can stop us now!"

Ella smiled. "Whatever Mrs. Brooks says, we can rescue animals and match the perfect pet with the perfect owner forever—can't we, Dad?"

"You bet," Dad said, giving first Ella then Caleb a high five. Then he snuck a look at Mom and Joel—a look that seemed to say, "Don't spoil the moment—let them enjoy it"—and the two grown-ups nodded back at him and drank from their glasses. Then Mom asked for the dessert menu.

"Apple pie," Ella decided. "With ice cream."

"Please," Dad reminded her.

"Please!"

"Double chocolate fudge cake with chocolate sauce." Caleb chose carefully from the list.

"Pl…" Dad began.

"Please!"

The waiter grinned as he took the order. "Looks like someone's celebrating," he said when he came back with their desserts.

Everybody nodded happily.

Munch, munch—sweet, tart apple pie—Ella was in dessert heaven! "I've got another great idea for the website," she announced between bites. "We should do a spring-clean-for-pets information thing—you know, how to get rid of fleas and tapeworms and stuff."

"Please!" Joel groaned. "Not while we're eating."

"Cool," Caleb said. "Did you know a single flea can lay up to 27 eggs per

day? We could give lots of information on how to get rid of them."

"Yuck, it's making me itch, even just thinking about it." But Joel knew when he was beaten by this animal-crazy family. He fell silent and dug into his strawberry ice cream.

Mom nodded. "You two can do the research then run it past me before you put it on the site."

"Great!" Caleb and Ella chorused.

Chapter Two
Daisy the Duckling

The next morning, a Saturday, Ella was up early.

"Come on, Cleo, let's go for a walk," she said to the young springer spaniel, who was raring to go.

Cleo jumped up at her kennel door. Along the row, other puppies and dogs wagged their tails and woofed.

"Later, Gus. Soon, Penny," Ella told the yappy Jack Russell and the elderly yellow Labrador. "I'll take you two for a walk after I've been down to the river with Cleo."

She slid the bolt to Cleo's door and the spaniel leaped out, racing down the aisle and bouncing up at the door that led out into the yard. "Slow down," Ella said with a shake of her head. She needed to get the dog on the leash in case she raced out into the road. "What's the hurry, Cleo?"

The spaniel jumped up, long ears flopping, short tail wagging.

"Sit!" Ella ordered. "Good girl." Quickly she clipped the leash onto Cleo's collar.

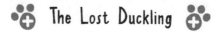

"Okay, now we can go."

Closing the door on the other dogs, Ella set off for the river. She held Cleo on a tight leash out of the yard and onto Main Street. She took a left down the side of Animal Magic along an overgrown path leading to stone steps and a path across fields to the nearby river. At the steps it was safe for Cleo to run free, so Ella let her off the leash.

"Wow, she sure can sprint!" she muttered as the dog bounded off through the long grass. "Heel, Cleo!" she called, seeing a young rabbit shoot out across the path with Cleo close behind.

The spaniel obeyed, ears drooping, tail tucked between her legs.

"Good girl," Ella told her. "No chasing baby rabbits, okay?"

They walked on for a while in the early morning sun. Blackbirds trilled in the hedges, and pigeons cooed from the nearby woods.

Soon Ella could hear the sound of water rippling over a stony bed, and when they turned the corner, they came out along the bank where the river bent in a wide arc. Nearby there was an old stone bridge and the smooth expanse of the golf course beyond.

"Okay, Cleo, now you can go and play," Ella said, pointing to a pebble bank and the cool, clear water.

With a yelp of joy Cleo went flying down to the river, nose down, following every delicious scent of the early summer morning. She sniffed here and there, at rabbit holes, molehills, and patches of scuffed earth, seizing a stick and bringing it to Ella, then darting back and waiting for it to be thrown.

"Fetch!" Ella called, flinging the stick as far as she could into the river.

The little spaniel plunged in and doggy-paddled toward the floating stick. She grabbed it and brought it back to shore.

"Hey!" Ella yelped as she bent to pick up the stick, ready to throw it again. Cleo had just shaken herself from head to toe. Icy droplets soaked Ella to the skin. But she threw the stick a second time and watched.

Cleo swam with her head just clear of the sparkling surface. She was a few feet from the stick, which was floating slowly downstream, when suddenly Ella saw the ducklings.

"Oh!" she said out loud, as the four little ducks paddled midstream. One after the other, they swam in a line— fluffy and yellow, heads up, battling the current. "Sweet!"

But where are their mom and dad? Ella wondered.

Woof! Spotting the ducklings, Cleo changed course and swam straight toward them.

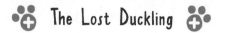

"Here, Cleo—heel!" Ella called.

This time the eager spaniel ignored her and made a beeline for the ducklings.

They were swimming against the current, too tiny to make much headway and scared stiff by the creature with the broad head and sharp white teeth that came closer and closer. *Cheep!* they cried. *Cheep-cheep!*

"Cleo, come back!" Ella shouted angrily.

Just then the ducklings' parents appeared from under the shelter of the far bank. They swam rapidly across the water, craning their necks and quacking loudly at Cleo.

"Bad dog, Cleo!" Ella yelled.

The spaniel turned her head. The

adult ducks were speeding toward her, flapping their wings, half-rising out of the water like angry jet-skiers.

Good for you! Ella thought, admiring the sleek green-black head of the male duck with its bright yellow beak, and the brown speckles of the female. *You tell Cleo off as much as you want—I don't blame you!*

Cheep-cheep! the ducklings cried. In their panic, they split off in four different directions.

Quack! The mother duck called them back. Three of them turned and swam straight to join her. But the fourth and smallest duckling—a ball of yellow fluff bobbing in the middle of the river— ignored her mother's call.

Meanwhile, the male attacked Cleo. He flew at her, flapping across the

23

water, stabbing at her with his beak and making a terrible racket.

Woof! Suddenly Cleo didn't like what she saw. She turned away from the lonely duckling and its angry dad and began swimming back to shore.

"That's right, come here!" Ella called.

Good riddance! The male duck followed, quacking angrily. Then, when he was sure Cleo had backed down, he turned and began to shoo the fourth duckling toward her brothers and sisters.

Cheep! The tiny cry sounded so cute.

Quack! said the angry dad.

"Thank goodness!" Ella sighed with relief to see the family back together. "Don't yell at the little one. She might be a bit skittish, but she was confused and didn't know what to do when Cleo suddenly appeared!"

Then, as quickly as the danger had begun, it was over. The spaniel was back onshore, shaking herself and drenching Ella. "Bad girl!" Ella said again, clipping Cleo's leash back on.

Cleo hung her head and tucked her tail between her legs.

Meanwhile, the four yellow ducklings were swimming with their parents toward the far bank. All was well.

"Daisy, Daisy duckling!" Ella made up a song as they walked back across the fields. "Bright yellow daffy-Daisy, silly little thing!" *Yes!* she thought, *Daisy! Daisy's a good name for the skittish one!*

She climbed the steps and walked quickly up the path. *I can't wait to tell everyone about Cleo and Daisy the duckling!*

Chapter Three

A Warm Welcome

"Oh, no, Ella's already given the duckling a name!" Caleb scoffed. "She's called it Daisy and now she's in love— again!"

"I am not!" Ella retorted. She'd been in the animal hospital, telling her mom all about the ducklings when her brother interrupted.

"Are!"

"Am not!"

"Hush, you two!" Mom warned,

picking up the phone. "Okay, Cathy, I can hear you now—yes, we do have a spare stable, so we can take Rosie—yes, right away then. Okay, 'bye!"

"I only said Daisy was cute!" Ella protested. "She's the littlest one, and she got separated from the others. Her big brave dad took care of her, though."

"How do you even know it's a she?" Caleb asked. While Ella had been out with Cleo, he'd been looking up flea facts and writing pages for the website. He'd discovered that fleas feed on blood. They lay eggs that drop from the pet onto the carpet and the furniture. "Did you know fleas prefer temperatures between 64 and 77 degrees?" he added.

"Yeah, I really needed to know that," Ella huffed. If Caleb wasn't going to show any interest in her ducklings, no way was she going to get excited about fleas.

"Mom, how many ducklings usually hatch in one nest?"

"Maybe six or seven," Mom said absentmindedly. She was busy jotting down numbers in a notebook. "Not all survive, though."

"That's sad! What happens to the ones who don't?"

"Oh, they're eaten by foxes maybe. Or they get separated from the rest before they're big enough to feed and take care of themselves. There are many dangers out there for a little duckling."

Ella shuddered. "Well, anyway, Daisy got safely back to her family before Cleo could do anything horrible, thank heavens."

Mom nodded.

"Daisy!" Caleb snorted, going back to his flea info.

"Ella, take Cleo into the kennels and rub her down with a towel. Then, if you like, you could come back and help me here." Mom closed her notebook and put on her pale-blue scrubs. She looked at her watch. "Almost time for the mad rush."

"I was going to take Gus and Penny for a walk," Ella told her.

"Oh, yeah, any excuse to go back and see the fluffy-wuffy ducklings!" Caleb grunted without turning around.

"Well, I don't mind," Mom shrugged. "But I thought you'd like to help me admit Rosie."

"Who's Rosie?" Ella asked.

"Rosie is a 12-year-old Shetland pony

who's looking for a home. I just took a phone call about her from Cathy Brown at Lucky Star Horse Rescue. Cathy rescued her a few weeks ago from a deserted campground just outside the city. From what she told me, the poor thing was practically starving."

"And is she okay now?" Ella asked, all thoughts of another dog walk, fleas, and ducklings quickly biting the dust.

Mom nodded. "Cathy fed her and got her back into good condition. Now she wants to hand her over to us. I said we'd find a home for Rosie, no problem."

"Cool!" Ella cried. "Which stable should we put her in? Should I lay a bed of fresh straw? Do Shetlands need special feed? What color is she?"

"Whoa!" Mom laughed. "You can

prepare the end stable next to Charlie the donkey if you'd like. And you can get Annie to help you."

Through the window Mom had spotted Annie Brooks running across the yard. Annie burst in through the door. "Hi, Mrs. Harrison, Hi, Caleb! Ella, do you want to come and ride Buttercup with me?"

"I'm sorry, Annie, but I'm too busy," Ella replied hurriedly. "We've got a new pony coming in." She disappeared down the hall to dry Cleo and put her into her kennel. When she came back, Annie was hovering behind Caleb, reading his newly created web page.

"Yuck!" Annie said. "Ewww! Fleas are attracted by your pet's body heat and movement. You can get skin diseases from them!"

"Enough about fleas!" Ella protested. "Annie, do you want to help me get the stable ready?"

"You bet!" Annie replied, racing out of the reception area ahead of Ella. "What kind of pony? When? What's its name?"

"A Shetland. Now. Rosie," Ella replied.

"Exciting!" Annie said.

Soon the girls were cutting the strings around a bale of straw and scattering the bedding. In the stable next door, Charlie the donkey scuffled his feet.

Caleb had given him his full name, Charlie Mouse, when he arrived at Animal Magic. "His coat is mouse-colored, and he has big ears. And anyway, Charlie Mouse suits him."

"Who says?" Ella had asked.

"I do," Caleb had replied.

"It's okay, Charlie, calm down," Ella soothed now. "You're going to have a new neighbor— someone you'll like, I promise!" She hung up a hay-net, then checked the water supply and the light switch. Everything was in working order.

"So when can we ride Buttercup?" Annie asked when the bed was laid.

She was eager to go out on her mom's beautiful gray mare.

"After Rosie gets here," Ella decided. "I can bring Penny and Gus with me and you can ride down the path to the river. With a bit of luck, we'll see Daisy."

Annie rested against the stable door. "Daisy who?" she asked.

And Ella was off again—"Daisy duckling—yellow and fluffy—cheep-cheep—so cute!"

It was almost midday before Cathy drove her trailer into the yard at Animal Magic. Meanwhile, Ella and Annie had been helping Joel in the hospital.

"What can we do while we're waiting

for Rosie?" Ella had asked.

"Plenty. You can wipe down the treatment tables for starters," Joel had said. Then he'd admitted a rabbit and told Ella to give Caleb information for the website.

"Hugo—a friendly, neutered brown rabbit. Litter-trained and likes to cuddle," Ella dictated.

Caleb had typed fast while Annie had taken a photo of the new admission.

Then they'd taken in a feral cat, found near the baseball field and brought in by the team captain, plus an unwanted hamster. The morning had flown.

"Here comes the Lucky Star trailer!" Caleb called just before twelve o'clock.

"At last!" Ella and Annie rushed out to greet it.

Cathy stepped down from her SUV. "Sorry I took so long," she apologized. "One of the ponies got a touch of colic. I had to call the vet."

"Can we see Rosie?" Ella asked, jumping up and down with excitement.

Cathy grinned. "Stand back while I lower the ramp and lead her out."

By this time, Mom, Joel, and Caleb had come out of the animal hospital and Dad had strolled out of the house, so there was a small crowd to meet Rosie.

They waited anxiously until Cathy emerged from the trailer, then there were gasps and soft cries of surprise.

"Oh, she's so small!"

"Tiny!"

"Sweet!"

Cathy led Rosie down the ramp. The

little Shetland was chocolate brown with a white flash on her nose and two white forelegs. Her heavy brown mane hung long and shaggy over her face and neck; her legs were short and stumpy.

"Nice round belly," Mom said with a grin. "Definitely no sign of her starving now!"

"Look at her little hooves!" Annie cried.

"Such a cute face!" Ella sighed.

Even Caleb joined in. "Yep, she's cool," he agreed. "I bet she's about as big as a Great Dane."

"Smaller!" Annie insisted. "Tiny, tiny!"

"Ella, would you lead her to her stable?" Cathy asked, handing over the rope.

Slowly and gently, Ella led Rosie into her new home. The others followed.

An inquisitive Charlie stuck his big, bony head over his door and stared down at Rosie. *Ee-aw!*

Rosie walked on by without a sideways glance. She'd smelled sweet hay in the hay-net and fresh, clean straw.

"She's pretty calm and relaxed considering how badly she's been treated," Cathy advised. "And of course she'll make a wonderful child's pony. You should put that on your website."

Ee-aw! Charlie insisted from next door.

Rosie took no notice and started to eat her hay, *munch-munch*.

"We'll put her on the website right away," Mom told Cathy. "And we'll let you know as soon as we find a good owner for her."

Munch-munch. Rosie rolled the hay around her mouth and ground it between her teeth.

Ee-aw! Charlie brayed.

Dad put his hands over his ears. "What a racket! I'm out of here!"

"Me, too," Joel agreed.

Gradually the stables emptied, until only Ella and Annie were left.

The two girls stared at Rosie with total delight.

"So can we ride Buttercup now?" Annie said at last.

"If we can tear ourselves away," Ella answered dreamily. She loved Rosie's dark brown eyes peering out from under the shaggy fringe.

"Buttercup needs the exercise," Annie reminded Ella.

"And I should walk Penny and Gus," Ella sighed. *If only Mom would let me keep Rosie!* But no, she knew that would never happen.

It was Annie's turn to sigh. "Come on, then—let's go."

"Yes, let's go."

They sighed again, but for the longest time neither Ella nor Annie moved.

Chapter Four
A Risky Crossing

"Steady, Buttercup, no need to push."
Annie reined her horse back to let Ella
open the gate. The two dogs, Gus and
Penny, ran ahead.

It was twelve-thirty, and at last the
two girls had torn themselves away
from beautiful Rosie.

"Lunch is at one-thirty!" Mrs. Brooks
had called over the fence as she heard
Annie set off for the river on Buttercup.
"Don't be late!"

They had an hour to walk the
dogs, exercise Buttercup, and see the
ducklings. "Go ahead, canter Buttercup
around the edge of the field," Ella told
Annie as she shut the gate. "I'll catch up
to you down by the river."

She took the dogs on a short cut and
arrived ahead of Annie, holding open
the next gate and letting them through.

"Your turn." Annie dismounted and offered Ella her riding helmet.

Quickly, Ella slid her foot into the stirrup and swung into the saddle. With a click of her tongue she headed the gray mare along the riverside path. "The ducklings were a little further along, around that bend in the river," she explained to Annie, who called Penny and Gus and put them on their leashes.

Leading the way, Ella kept her eyes peeled. "Watch out for the golfers!" she called over her shoulder as across the river, a player struck a ball high into the air and Ella watched it plop safely onto the green.

Penny and Gus barked at the ball, desperate to chase after it.

"Sorry you two," Annie said. "You

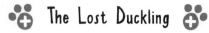

have to stay on your leashes."

"The ducklings were around here somewhere, swimming in the middle of the river," Ella told Annie. "I can't see them yet—no, they're not here—oh, yes, there they are!"

Sure enough, a group of baby ducks appeared at the edge of the river, paddling among the reeds, while two adults swam further out from the bank, keeping a careful lookout.

"One, two, three, four ... five!" Ella counted the ducklings. She looked again. "Hey, this must be a different family. Yes, the ducklings are bigger, which means they're a little older than the ones I saw this morning. They have more brown speckles...."

"They're still cute," Annie said with a

smile. She kept tight hold of the dogs and watched the ducklings splash and dive. "Look at that one chasing after its mother. Its little legs are paddling like crazy!"

"But where's Daisy?" Ella wondered. "If you saw her, you'd really be talking cute!"

Walking Buttercup slowly along the riverbank, she kept a lookout for her first and favorite duckling family. She saw a tiny black-and-white bird skim the surface of the sparkling water, then veer off toward the golf course.

"Hey, Ella!" Annie called, pointing to the far bank. "Is that them?"

And there they were—four little yellow ducklings following their sleek brown mother up the steep bank onto the smooth grass of the golf course.

The mom waddled ahead, her flat, webbed feet placed firmly on the ground. The little ones followed, stopping and starting, lowering their heads to nip at blades of grass, then scooting quickly to catch up with their mom.

"Oh, yes! Look, Daisy's the little one in the back!" Ella cried, jumping down from the saddle and letting Buttercup drop her head to graze. "Uh-oh, she can't get up the slope—oh, yes, she can—go on, Daisy, you can make it!"

"She's getting left behind!" Annie said, willing Daisy to scramble up the bank. "Hey, wait for her!" she called to the others.

The tiny duckling struggled to catch up.

"Why are they heading across the

golf course?" Annie wanted to know. "Shouldn't they stay by the river?"

Ella shrugged. "I don't know. And I don't think those golfers have seen them either. If they're not careful they'll hit the balls straight at the ducklings!"

On went the mother duck, marching across the green. One, two, three—the bigger ducklings followed. Four! Finally Daisy made it onto the golf course.

Whack! The first golfer hit a ball onto the green. *Thud!* It landed about 30 feet from Ella's family of ducklings. Their mother quacked and ran back to herd her offspring into a tight huddle.

"I've got to warn those golfers!" Ella decided. She waved her arms and shouted. "Excuse me! Can you wait a few minutes before you hit the next ball?"

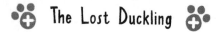

The three men looked across the river and frowned at the two girls with a horse and two dogs. "What was that you said?" one yelled back.

"Can you wait until the ducks have gotten across the green?" Ella repeated. Then she remembered her manners. "Please!"

"Ducks?" the same man echoed. "Where?"

"There!" Ella pointed to the mother duck and her brood. "Your golf balls are scaring them!"

The man turned to his two companions, who shook their heads and stood with hands on hips.

"Oops!" Annie muttered. "They don't look happy."

"Neither does Daisy." Ella saw her favorite duckling cower in the middle of the bunch. Then the mother duck flapped her wings and quickly began to hustle the ducklings back down toward the river.

"That's right," Annie muttered. "Get out of their way!"

"Hang on, I'm sure they won't take long!" Ella called to the golfers.

"Can't believe we have to stop play because of a bunch of silly ducks!" one of them grumbled.

Soon, though, the mother managed to get her ducklings across the open green and into the long grass of the riverbank.

"It's okay now!" Ella called. "Thanks!"

"Phew!" Annie sighed. "And look, here comes the dad!"

Just then the male flew low along the course of the river. He beat his wings strongly, swooping down and landing in the water with a splash. With a loud quack he called for his family to join him. And out came the mother duck with her babies. Daisy was last as usual, cheeping and bobbing in the rough water, struggling to keep up.

"I hope Daisy doesn't get left behind again," Annie muttered, watching another family of ducks swim out from the bank.

"Oh, dear, I don't think the two families get along." Ella noticed the males stretch out their necks and flap their wings. The females, too, were

making a lot of noise, leaving their babies and standing up on their legs with their wings outstretched to warn each other off.

Annie looked at her watch. "Uh-oh, it's almost one-thirty. I'm going to be late. Come on, Penny, up you get. Time to go home, Gus!" Quickly she led the dogs back along the path.

Lingering only to make sure that Daisy had caught up with her brothers and sisters, Ella swung up into Buttercup's saddle and headed for home. "What did you think of Daisy?" she called to Annie, who had hurried ahead.

"Totally cute!" Annie agreed.

Ella smiled as Buttercup trod steadily along the track. "You know what," she decided, talking more to herself than to Annie. "I'm going to write about Daisy and her family on Animal Magic's website—where they live, what they eat, how quickly they grow up, stuff like that."

"A blog!" Annie nodded. "That's a great idea!"

Ella grinned and urged Buttercup on toward home. "Yes, I'm going to start an online duckling diary!"

Chapter Five
Duckling Diary

<u>Sunday the 13th.</u> Went out with Cleo twice, down to the river. Didn't see Daisy. Spotted the family of older ducklings, though. Five of them with Mom. No sign of Daisy and the others, boo-hoo.

<u>Monday the 14th.</u> School today, so couldn't go down to the river until after school. Still no Daisy duckling. Typical! Just because I decide to write this blog, she vanishes!

Ella closed the laptop and sighed. The missing duckling wasn't the only thing on her mind. Earlier that day she'd heard Mom talking to Dad—something about donations to Animal Magic being down last month and not having enough money to pay some bills. Her mom had looked worried and had stopped talking the moment she'd seen Ella.

It wasn't fair! Just when they had received the good news from the Council, it seemed that there was something new to worry about.

<u>Tuesday the 15th.</u> No Daisy! Miss Elliot came to Annie's house to visit Buttercup and Chance. Hope I see Daisy tomorrow.

Late that night, tucked in bed, Ella thought about what she'd put on her blog. It had been a busy few days at Animal Magic. Blossom the feral cat had been quickly adopted. Three people had already been over to look at Rosie. A family named Whitaker said they were very interested in offering her a home. Gus the terrier had been adopted by Pete Knight, one of the volunteers who had helped her dad build the stable block.

So Ella hadn't had much time to look for Daisy or to keep a record in her blog.

"Anyway, there's nothing to write about!" she sighed as she settled down to sleep. She lay awake for a while, thinking of little Daisy bobbing on the water and remembering what her mom

had said a few days before. "Not all ducklings survive.... They're eaten by foxes ... or they get separated.... There are many dangers out there for a little duckling."

What if Daisy has gotten lost?

"Still awake?" Mom asked, popping her head around Ella's door when she came up to bed herself.

Ella nodded.

Her mom came to sit on the edge of her bed. "Worried about something?"

"I haven't seen Daisy in such a long time," Ella confessed. "The last time was when I was with Annie and some golfers almost whacked their ball straight at the ducklings! Plus, there was another family of ducks, and the grown-ups were arguing, plus...."

"Whoa!" Mom shushed her. "Ella, ducks are territorial. They like to have their own stretch of riverbank, or an area on a pond, like most other animals. If there's more than one family by the bridge, it's likely that one has been chased off elsewhere. That's probably what happened to Daisy and her family."

Ella listened and nodded. "That's most likely the reason why the mother duck was herding Daisy and the others up the bank over the golf course—she was looking for somewhere else to live."

"Exactly. Which is the reason you haven't seen Daisy lately," her mom agreed.

"But what if she got left behind?" Ella said, still worried. "I mean, she's so little and she could easily get separated and lost...."

Mom shook her head. "I think you're worrying more than you need. Daisy is probably safe with her family, tucked away in a nice new stretch of riverbank, and busily settling into her new home!"

Deciding to extend her search the next day, Ella lay for a while in silence.

"Mom," she said after a while.

"Mmm?"

"What were you and Dad talking about yesterday—you know, something to do with money and stuff?"

"Nothing for you to worry about," Mom replied, gently patting Ella's hand.

"Is it about Animal Magic?" Ella persisted. "Are we running out of money to run our rescue center?"

"Oh, Ella." Mom gently pushed Ella's hair back from her face. "Money is always a struggle, it's true. We're a charity, so we rely on gifts and voluntary contributions. But you and Caleb have to let your dad and me take care of that side of things. That's what grown-ups do!"

Slowly, Ella nodded. "Mom…," she began after another long pause. She was feeling sleepy at last, drifting off, with just one more question to ask.

"Yes?"

"If we run out of money, will we have to close Animal Magic, even though we got the good news from the Council?"

"Let's not worry about that right now," Mom replied. "It's time to get some sleep."

Wednesday the 16th. Walked over the old bridge and searched further down the riverbank. Still no Daisy! Am worried, even though Mom said not to be. Where is she? Is she lost and all alone? What happened to her and her family?

The Whitaker family said no to Rosie in the end because it turns out they might be moving to a new house. Daisy, Daisy, where are you?

On Thursday afternoon, Ella had come out of school with a load of homework. But instead of getting on the bus as usual, her dad had picked her and Caleb up in his delivery van and driven them home.

"Good day?" Dad had asked, and Caleb had told him that Jake Harwood's mom had said yes to Ernie the hamster and they were coming to Animal Magic to see him right after school.

Ella sat quietly, staring out of the window as the houses of the city gradually gave way to fields. *Math homework—yuck! English—read chapters 6 and 7 in the textbook.*

Walk Penny before dinnertime. Walk Cleo after. Look for Daisy again.

"Ella?" Dad asked. "Hey, daydreamer, did you hear what I just said?"

Ella gave a small start. She recognized the edge of Crystal Park—they were passing the end of Three Oaks Road, then Arbor Court. "What? No."

"I said that the sale of Miss Elliot's old house has just gone through. She called the rescue center earlier today to tell Mom."

"Is that good?" Ella asked. She remembered the time when Caleb had climbed a tree in the yard of Miss Elliot's ancient manor house and rescued the elderly lady's tabby cat, Tigger.

Soon after that, Miss Elliot had decided the house was too much for her and had moved to a smaller place in Arbor Court. Animal Magic had taken in her pregnant gray mare, Buttercup, which was where her handsome foal, Chance, had been born. Then Mrs. Brooks had fallen in love with Buttercup and Chance, and she'd forgiven Animal Magic for all the animal noises and extra traffic they'd brought to town.

"It's very good news," Dad told Ella now. "I'm happy for her. Miss Elliot is relieved it's all over and she has the money from the sale of her house. No more money worries for that lady, at least."

"Cool," Ella said absentmindedly.

Then, as they drove up Main Street, closer to home, she suddenly yelled, "Dad, watch out! Stop, Dad, stop!"

There, right in front of them, was the last thing she'd expected to see—two ducks and four ducklings marching in single file straight across the street!

Dad glanced in his mirror, then slammed on the brakes. The van swerved slightly toward the pavement then stopped. "Everyone okay?" he asked.

Caleb nodded.

"It's Daisy!" Ella cried. "Look—the little one at the back. She's not lost after all—that's Daisy!"

Hop-skip-hop—the fluffy yellow bundle scrambled to keep up.

"Narrow escape," Caleb muttered. "Can I get out and shoo them onto the side of the road?"

Dad gave the go-ahead. "Watch out for traffic," he warned.

Waddle-waddle—the adult ducks took no notice of the van and made their way steadily from one side of the road to the other.

Caleb jumped out. "Shoo!" he called, making a whooshing, herding gesture with his arms. "Go on, shoo!"

Ella glanced anxiously up and down the road. Luckily, there were no other cars around—only George Stevens, Caleb's friend, riding by on his bike. He stopped to let Caleb herd the ducks safely across the road.

"What are they doing here?" Ella asked, still hardly able to believe her eyes.

Waddle-waddle, hop-skip-hop. The road was hard, gray, and wide for the tiny ducklings.

"I have no idea," Dad replied. He waited until Caleb had finished the job and told George what was going on.

"We almost ran them over!" Caleb

reported. "Honestly, talk about bird-brained!"

"That's not fair," Ella muttered. "You can't blame the ducks!"

"No, they don't know any better. But a busy road is a pretty dangerous place to go walking around," her dad pointed out. "Let's hope they don't try it again."

Ella frowned but stayed silent as Caleb jumped back in the van and her dad drove the last few blocks home. Her head was buzzing—not about math or walking the dogs—it was about Daisy and what else she, Ella, could do to make sure Daisy and her family were safer on the road.

Chapter Six
Wildlife Watch

<u>Thursday the 17th.</u> Major traffic panic. Daisy and her family tried to cross the main road and we almost ran them over! <u>***They're not by the riverbank anymore; they're living on the big pond behind Arbor Court.***</u> This is how I found out—Dad picked us up from school and as we drove along, they were crossing the road with Daisy lagging behind as usual. Dad braked and we missed them.
The minute we got home, I went back to look for them. I asked Miss Elliot

if she'd seen the ducklings on the road because she was sitting in her yard with Tigger when it happened. She said yes, she had watched it all. Then she saw the adult ducks lead the ducklings on down the street. They actually crossed her yard and went into the field in the back!
So I climbed over Miss Elliot's fence and followed the ducks to the pond. It belongs to Mr. and Mrs. Wheeler. They own a big house with a tennis court and a pond and everything.
So Daisy has a new home, not by the river anymore. And Mrs. Wheeler says I can visit the pond anytime I want to keep an eye on her. Phew!
But in any case, Caleb and I decided to make a sign for the road just in case the ducks go back that way again. "SLOW DOWN—DUCKS CROSSING!" in giant red letters.
We stuck the cardboard sign on a

wooden stake and hammered it into
the grass. Hope it works.
Didn't have time to do English
homework. Hope Mom will write a note
for Miss Jennings so I don't get in
trouble. Fingers crossed.
***Daisy's safe and she's not lost.
How cool is that!***

"So, Rosie, I got into big trouble with
Miss Jennings today," Ella told the
Shetland pony. It was Friday evening,
and Charlie the donkey was noisily
chewing hay in the stable next door.
"Mom wouldn't write me a note. She
said making the DUCKS CROSSING!
sign wasn't a good enough excuse for me
not doing my homework. Is that mean
or what!"

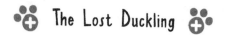

Rosie nuzzled Ella's hand, looking for a treat. Her long, shaggy forelock completely covered her eyes.

"How do you see through all that hair?" Ella wondered, gently pushing the mane to one side. "So anyway, I tried to explain, but Miss Jennings gave me a big speech about how schoolwork should always come first, no matter what. In front of the entire class! In the end she gave me extra work, which I now have to hand in, plus the homework on Monday morning!"

Life was tough, Ella decided, though Rosie didn't seem to care. Instead, she wandered over to her hay-net and began to munch.

"Ah, here you are!" Miss Elliot interrupted as Ella leaned against Rosie's stable door, her chin resting on the top. "Your mother said I might find you here."

Ella swung around to face the elderly

lady. "Why, has something happened?" she asked anxiously. "Is Daisy okay?"

"Yes, yes," Miss Elliot smiled. "That's what I came to tell you—I was looking out of my bedroom window earlier this afternoon, and I saw the entire family swimming on the Wheelers' pond. They look as if they've settled nicely."

"That's wonderful!" Ella heaved a sigh of relief. She was grateful to Miss Elliot for coming to tell her. "I'd like to come down and see Daisy, if that's okay with you."

Another smile and a nod. "Of course, my dear. That's what Mom guessed you'd say, so I told her I'd keep a careful eye on you while you take a look down by the pond."

"Okay." Feeling like a toddler in need of a babysitter, Ella went with Miss Elliot

across the yard and out onto Main Street. Still, she knew the elderly lady meant well.

"Your sign seems to be working," Miss Elliot pointed out as two cars slowed down almost to a halt. "Drivers certainly seem to be reading it."

"Cool," Ella noted. "It was my idea—just in case the ducks try to get back to the river."

"Very thoughtful," Miss Elliot agreed.

She and Ella passed the sign and turned into Arbor Crescent and the neat row of houses with their small front yards. They found Tigger sitting patiently on the front doorstep, waiting for his owner to return.

As Miss Elliot invited Ella into her yard, she gave a small click of her

tongue, as if hesitating over what she was about to say. "Tell me, dear, is your mother well?"

The question surprised Ella. "She's fine, thanks," she said.

"She looked a little pale. And she didn't seem her usual cheerful self," Miss Elliot went on.

"She's been pretty busy," Ella replied, trying to scan the field at the back of Miss Elliot's house to catch sight of Daisy and her family on the pond. "And she didn't get much sleep. Last night someone called her at midnight to say they'd gotten back home from their vacation and heard an animal whining and growling inside their garage. The woman was too scared to open the door, so Mom had to go and find out what was trapped inside.

"It turned out it was a stray dog—a cross-breed that got in and couldn't get out again. It had almost starved to death while the woman was away. Mom brought the dog straight back to Animal Magic."

"I certainly do admire your mother," Miss Elliot told Ella. "But are you sure that nothing is worrying her?"

Ella shrugged. "Only the usual stuff about trying to pay bills and not having enough money," she admitted. "But that's nothing new for us at Animal Magic."

"Your mother does amazingly good work." Miss Elliot nodded her head and took a deep breath, as if she'd just come to a big decision. "Now, I expect you're wanting to go down to the pond for a

closer look at your ducklings," she said
to Ella.

"Yes, please."

"Well, wait here a second while I get
my binoculars for you. You'll get a
much better, close-up view if you use
them."

So Ella took the binoculars, then
climbed the fence and trod carefully
through the long grass.

"Everything's blurry!" she muttered,
putting the binoculars to her eyes. Then
she twisted a metal knob, which altered
the lenses so that the scene grew clear.

Zoom! The binoculars gave her a
close-up of the pond with its long,
straight reeds at the edge and small,
rocky island in the center. "Wow!" Ella
was impressed.

From the middle of the field she
could easily pick out three Canada
geese standing on the island and a
small, white crane standing to one side.
She walked steadily on, aiming the
binoculars at other wildlife—a rabbit
scuttling off across the field, and up in

the blue sky, three large birds soaring on an air current.

This is what it must be like to make films about wildlife! Ella thought. She swung back to the pond and saw three more cranes in the shallow water, standing among the reeds. *This is exciting!*

Two geese swam into view from around the back of the island. That made five altogether. Ella crept closer, then settled by the edge of the pond. From this distance she could make out the long black necks and brown speckled wings of the geese. *Just think, if this was Africa, I'd be looking at pink flamingos! Or I could go to India and film tigers!* She zoomed in on the cranes.

That's it. I'm going to be a wildlife filmmaker when I grow up!

Ella's imagination took off and soared as high as the birds overhead. It was only when she spotted her first duck that she came back to earth.

It was the male with his bright blue-green neck feathers and white collar, his plumage shining in the sunlight.

Perfect! Ella thought, holding her breath.

Then came the female—rounder, plump and proud, with her head up, swimming out from behind the island after the male.

Okay, where are the ducklings? Ella kept her binoculars fixed on the spot. One duckling swam into view, bright yellow and perky. Then the second, bold and happy. The third took his time, but finally swam out from behind the rock.

Mom, Dad, and ducklings 1, 2, and 3.

"Come on, Daisy!" Ella muttered. With binoculars steady in her hands, she waited a long time for her fluffy favorite to appear. And waited. And waited.

Chapter Seven
The Lost Duckling

Friday the 18th. ***Daisy's lost. She's missing.*** I borrowed Miss Elliot's binoculars and waited by the pond for a really long time. There was no sign of her.

Ella sat with the rescue center's laptop on her knees. She'd written the truth and now it hit her really hard.

Her mom came into the bedroom to ask her to turn off her light. "Everything

yellow ball of fluff. "Well, I haven't given up!" she said stubbornly.

Her mom put an arm around her shoulder and gave her a hug. "So what next?" she asked.

Now suddenly Ella knew exactly what she was going to do. She closed the laptop and snuggled under her comforter. "It's Saturday tomorrow," she said. "I'm going to go out first thing in the morning to look for Daisy!"

Ella got up early as promised. She dressed and put on her sneakers, ready to go out and start her search.

There's no point going back to the pond at Arbor Court, she thought, skipping breakfast and setting off on foot in the direction of the river. *I spent a long time there yesterday with the binoculars, and there was definitely no sign of her.*

So Ella decided to search the riverbank, close to where she'd first seen Daisy.

She crunched across pebbles and poked around in the tall reeds without finding anything. Then she crossed the stone bridge and started to look among the bushes at the edge of the golf course.

"Hey, you there! What do you think you're doing?" a voice called.

Ella glanced up to see an angry golfer walking toward her.

"Don't you know you're trespassing?" the man shouted.

Reluctantly Ella broke off her search. "I'm trying to find a lost duckling," she explained. "Her name's Daisy. She got separated from her family."

"That doesn't change the fact that you're on private property," he argued. "What's more, you just put me off my game!"

Sighing, Ella retreated back over the bridge. She wandered further along the bank. "Where are you, Daisy?" she muttered, crouching to peer under the low branches of a willow tree. "Please don't hide. It's me—Ella. I'm your friend!"

But there were no answering cheeps, and no sign of the little lost duckling.

So Ella trudged back home, her head
hanging, her spirits low. It was almost
ten o'clock when she reached the house
and the phone was ringing. Ella ran to
answer it.

It was Miss Elliot. "Is this Ella?" she
asked hurriedly. "I'm glad I've caught
you."

"What's wrong?" Ella could tell from
the elderly lady's voice that something
bad had happened. Maybe Tigger was
sick. "Is everything okay?" she asked.

"No, dear, I'm afraid it's not!" Miss
Elliot answered. "It's Tigger...."

Just as Ella had thought! "Is he hurt?
Should I get Mom?" she cut in.

"No, wait a moment. I'm looking out
of my window to make sure. Yes, I was
right. Tigger is chasing a yellow bird in

my yard, and I'm too slow to stop him!"

"Is it a duckling?" Ella asked, her heart thumping, dreading the answer.

"I'm not absolutely sure," Miss Elliot reported breathlessly. "I can't see it clearly. I just caught a glimpse. Wait—Tigger is prowling across the lawn as we speak. He's definitely stalking…."

"Is it Daisy?" Ella interrupted.

"Come here, Tigger, you naughty boy!" Miss Elliot's voice grew fainter, then she came back to the phone. "Yes, it's definitely a duckling," she admitted. "You'd better come quickly, Ella, if you want to save your little friend!"

Chapter Eight
The Great Chase

Miss Elliot greeted Ella at her front gate. "I'm so sorry!" she gasped.

Ella's heart missed a beat. She was too late. It was all over and Tigger had done his worst!

"I can't stop Tigger from chasing birds. It's a terrible habit, I know!"

"Where is he?" Ella asked, bracing herself for what she would find.

"In the back yard, prowling among the rose bushes. I can't see the duckling...."

Ella nodded. There was still hope then. She sprinted around the side of the house to find the tabby cat crouched low on the ground, staring intently into the thick bushes beyond the roses.

"Shoo!" Ella cried, waving her arms and rushing at Tigger.

The cat twitched his tail but didn't take his eyes off the bushes.

"Go away! Shoo!" Ella yelled.

Tigger looked around. He glared angrily at Ella for disturbing him.

Meanwhile, there was a tiny movement from underneath the bushes, and Ella saw a speck of yellow between the green leaves.

Tigger turned back toward the bushes and pounced.

"Stop!" Ella cried. She realized there

was nothing she could do except to make a dive and grab the cat.

So as Tigger vanished under the bushes, Ella also pounced. Rose thorns pricked her bare wrists as she threw herself forward. The landing was hard, but she barely felt it. "Got you!" she muttered as she seized Tigger and pulled him out from the bottom of the bushes.

"Great job! Good girl!" Miss Elliot clapped her hands.

Taking a deep breath, Ella quickly handed a squirming Tigger to the elderly lady. Then she went down on her hands and knees and crawled back under the bushes. "So this is where you went, Daisy!" she muttered, parting the slim branches and catching sight of the tiny duckling cowering in the shadows.

Cheep-cheep-cheep! Daisy scrambled among the tangled roots, out of Ella's reach.

"Don't worry, I'm not going to hurt you," she promised, stretching forward to cup the duckling between her hands.

But Daisy didn't understand. Scared out of her wits by the fierce cat, all she wanted to do was run and hide.

She struggled deep into the bushes and disappeared again.

"Come back!" Ella pleaded, hearing Miss Elliot take Tigger inside the house. "Don't run away. You're safe now. I'm here to take you back to your family!"

Back to the pond at Arbor Court, to her brothers and sisters and the safety of her mom and dad.

Gently, Ella parted more branches. Her wrists were specked with blood from the rose thorns and beginning to sting.

"Ella, what on earth are you doing?"

Annie's voice interrupted Ella's careful search. She sounded like her mother in a bad mood. Without answering, Ella continued looking for Daisy.

"Ella, I can see your legs and feet, so I know you're under there!" Annie insisted.

"I saw you sprint off down Main Street. I followed to find out what you were up to."

"Be quiet, Annie!" Ella hissed. Every second that passed meant she had less of a chance of saving Daisy. By now she'd totally lost sight of the duckling and was starting to fear that Daisy had disappeared for good.

"But you have to tell me what happened." In her own way, Annie was as stubborn as Ella. "Come out. I want to know."

Miss Elliot hurried out of the house to explain. "Tigger was stalking Ella's missing duckling. We almost had a disaster on our hands."

"Please be quiet!" Ella pleaded. All this talking was going to scare Daisy away.

Miss Elliot lowered her voice to a

whisper. "I brought out the binoculars in case they can help," she told Annie. "You wait here with them. I'll go back inside and make sure Tigger doesn't try to escape. He's very angry about being locked in."

Annie nodded. "Can you see Daisy?" she asked Ella quietly.

"No. She was here a few moments ago," Ella sighed. Her arms were really hurting now and her hair was getting caught in twigs. "Ouch! Hang on, I need to take a break."

She emerged from the bushes, a bedraggled mess.

Ella picked the leaves off her sweater, noting Annie's smoothly brushed hair and whiter than white T-shirt. "She was here, but I think I lost her," she admitted miserably.

"Let me look," Annie offered, handing Ella the binoculars and crawling through the rose bushes. She peered into the dark undergrowth. "Nothing," she reported at last, emerging with tousled hair and gray dirt on her T-shirt.

Ella raised her eyebrows. Now they both looked a mess.

Annie sighed and wiped her hands on her T-shirt. Then she noticed Miss Elliot holding Tigger under her arm and tapping at the window.

"Come quickly!" the elderly lady mouthed through the glass.

The girls ran to the back door.

"I saw the duckling!" Miss Elliot gasped. "Out on the pavement in front of the house next door. Once Tigger was

out of the way, she must have fled across my neighbor's yard. She's heading for Main Street!"

Ella didn't stop to think. She simply ran out onto the driveway and picked up the search. "Daisy!" she shouted, running up the street, hoping yet afraid she would find the duckling walking down the street. So much unknown danger, so many disasters waiting to happen in the big wide world!

"Daisy!" she called again as she reached Main Street and stopped by the sign reading SLOW DOWN—DUCKS CROSSING!

Annie sprinted to join her. "It's practically deserted," she gasped, looking both ways and praying that cars didn't speed by.

In the distance a tractor rumbled up

the street. Pete Knight was out walking
Gus. He gave the girls a wave.

"Hey, Pete, have you seen a stray
duckling?" Ella called, not knowing
which way to turn.

Pete thought for a moment. "I was
going to say no, but come to think of it,
maybe we did."

Ella and Annie ran up to him. "What happened?" Annie asked.

"I just had to give Gus a stern talking to," Pete explained. "He was trying to run off down the street at the side of your place, Ella. I wanted him to keep going straight ahead. It's a good thing I had him on the leash."

Ella glanced down at the lively terrier and gave him a pat. "So?" she asked.

"So I wondered what was so interesting down the road and took a quick look. I didn't see anything, but it could have been a small animal or bird that Gus had spotted. Maybe even your duckling."

"Okay, thanks, Pete. Come on, Annie!" Ella didn't wait to hear more. It was the only lead they had, and she was determined to follow it.

"Are you thinking what I'm thinking?" Annie asked breathlessly as they sped down the narrow road.

Ella nodded. "It would make sense for Daisy to make her way back to the river, wouldn't it? I mean, she'd recognize Main Street and the turn down this road. She'd be thinking she might find her mom and dad down here."

"Poor thing!" Annie gasped. She glanced helplessly in the long grass. "Maybe we should slow down and take a closer look."

"You do that. I'll run on ahead to search by the river."

Ella sprinted on with the binoculars until she reached the riverbank.

She kept a sharp lookout every step
of the way but saw no sign of the
yellow duckling. *So many places to hide!*
she thought, almost overcome by
the difficulty of the search. One tiny
duckling, one great big countryside!

Stopping by the bend in the river,
Ella raised the binoculars and focused
them. Soon she could pick out pink
wildflowers growing on the banks and
individual pebbles on the shore.

She scanned the scene for a long
time. Behind her she could hear Annie's
footsteps coming closer.

"Anything?" Annie called.

"Nothing so far. How about you?"

"Zilch. It's a long way down that
path. Do you think Daisy would get
this far?"

Ella nodded. "She's done it once already."

"But not by herself."

"I know. Wait a sec." Ella steadied the binoculars. Across the far side of the river she spotted a pair of ducks swimming out from the bank. "See over there!" she told Annie. Could it be Daisy's mom and dad, back in their old stretch of river to search for their missing duckling?

The ducks swam boldly midstream.

No, they wouldn't leave their other babies, Ella thought. The binoculars brought out every detail of the male's shining neck feathers and yellow beak, even his beady eyes.

"Look." Annie pointed to the bank. "Here come the ducklings!"

One—two—three—four … five! Annie and Ella held their breath and counted.

The speckled ducklings headed straight for their parents until the entire family was happily bobbing in the rippling water.

"Those are the ducks that chased Daisy's family away," Ella muttered. She lowered the binoculars and handed them to Annie.

It took Annie a while to get used to them. At first all she saw was a blur of sky and grass. Then she got the hang of it. "Wow, that's clear!" she said.

But Ella didn't hear her. She'd wandered off down to the pebbly shore and was looking left and right, feeling almost hopeless when it happened. "Oh!" she gasped.

"What?" Annie asked, turning sharply.

Ella hadn't believed it at first, but now she was sure—a tiny yellow creature had emerged from the long grass onto the gray pebbles. It was hopping and scrambling toward the water with a faint cheeping sound.

Annie stopped and stared.

"Daisy duckling!" Ella whispered with a sudden surge of hope. "You're amazing! You made it back to the river all by yourself!"

Chapter Nine
Pond Danger

Daisy fluttered clumsily toward the river.

Ella and Annie watched in helpless silence.

"What do we do?" Annie whispered.

Ella shook her head. "I don't know. If we make a move, we'll scare her," Ella muttered under her breath.

"She's all alone," Annie said softly. "Oh look, she's starting to swim toward the other ducks!"

"But they won't want her," Ella

predicted. "She doesn't belong to them, and my mom said that ducks are very territorial."

Sure enough, as Daisy swam bravely out into the strong current, the mother duck spied her and gave a warning quack. The dad circled around his babies and gathered them in a tight knot.

"Come back, Daisy!" Annie begged.

But the little lone duckling swam on.

Quack! The mother duck's warnings grew louder. She swam toward Daisy, who was still struggling against the current. Then she stopped to tread water, watching carefully.

Cheep-cheep! Little Daisy swam right up to the female duck, asking to be taken in.

Quack! The angry mother stabbed at

Daisy with her broad beak to chase her away.

"Oh, that's cruel!" Annie cried.

"Daisy, come back here," Ella begged.

But Daisy tried again—swimming up close and dodging the stabbing beak, coming back a third time and being chased away.

"It's awful!" Ella wailed. "You'd think the mother duck would take pity on Daisy!"

"Sad!" Annie cried.

"Who's sad?" Caleb interrupted. He'd been walking along the riverbank with the old Labrador, Penny, when he'd spotted the anxious girls. "What are you two up to?"

"It's Daisy!" Ella pointed to the middle of the river, where the female duck was still angrily sending the duckling away. "She's desperate for this other family to adopt her, but they're shooing her off. Look, now the male duck's joining in!"

"That's not good." Caleb frowned. "I'll tell you what—let me send Penny in to scare the adults."

He didn't wait for Ella and Annie to make up their minds. Instead, he picked up a large stick and threw it into the river for the Labrador. "Penny, fetch!" he ordered.

The dog plunged into the water and swam strongly after the stick. As soon as the ducks saw her, they quacked and quickly turned the other way.

"Don't hurt Daisy!" Ella cried after Penny.

Daisy was stranded mid-river, paddling bravely but making no headway. Meanwhile, the unwelcoming ducks had fled to the far bank.

"Good girl, Penny!" Caleb called. "Hey, look at them scatter!"

"That's enough," Annie said. "Call Penny back before she grabs one of them."

Caleb nodded. "Okay. Here, Penny!"

The obedient Labrador turned tail and paddled back to the riverbank, while lonely Daisy seemed to give up the struggle at last and allowed herself to be carried downstream.

Just then, another duck appeared, flying low along the course of the river, under the arch of the stone bridge.

"Hey!" Ella pointed. She took the binoculars from Annie and tried to focus on Daisy, but the duck was quickly out of sight. *I wonder!*

There was no time to stop and think. Daisy was being swept away toward the bridge.

"Let's run down there," Caleb decided. "Maybe Daisy will manage to get back onto the bank where the river bends and we can rescue her."

As he and the wet dog sprinted off, Ella and Annie decided to follow. "I feel so sorry for Daisy!" Annie muttered. "I have this awful feeling that she's not going to make it."

"Don't say that!" Ella cried. Her heart was in her mouth as she ran along the bank, watching Daisy bob and turn in the swirling water.

Caleb and Penny were ahead, leaning over the bridge, watching the duckling come toward them. Annie and Ella were directly across from Daisy. They saw her begin to swim again and fight the current. Gradually she made progress toward their bank.

"See, she's a little fighter!" Ella said.

And now the same new duck was flying back, swooping low, skimming the surface of the water as it slowed and flew smoothly under the old bridge, quacking to draw the tiny duckling's attention.

Daisy looked up and cheeped loudly.

The duck flew past, then with a tilt of her strong wings she turned and came back yet again.

Daisy swam toward the pebbles where Annie and Ella stood. Both girls held their breath. From the bridge Caleb crossed his fingers and watched.

Swoop! Splash! The duck landed in the water with a trail of spray. She swam right up to Daisy, guiding her out of the water onto the shore, fussing and flapping her wings as if to say, *There you are, you silly girl! I thought I told you never to leave my side!*

"It's Daisy's mom!" Annie cried in total joy. "She came back to find her baby!"

On the bridge Caleb smiled and nodded.

Ella stared at Daisy and her mother, too choked up to say a word.

Chapter Ten

A Generous Gift

<u>Saturday the 19th.</u> ...And guess what—
Mother Duck marched Daisy up the
riverbank and straight up the road!
There was just this bossy female
and one tiny duckling making their
way between the bushes like little
soldiers marching, left—right—left.
We followed them every step of the
way, but the two ducks took no
notice. They went up by the side of
Animal Magic onto Main Street, past
the DUCKS CROSSING! sign, and left
into Arbor Court. Miss Elliot was
so surprised when she saw it. She'd

been waiting at her window all that time, making sure that Tigger didn't get out and cause more trouble.

But Daisy and her mom didn't stop. They waddled across the yard and under the fence, right across the field. We could just see the mom's head popping up over the grass. (We had to keep a safe distance so we wouldn't scare them.)

The best part was when they reached their pond. Daddy Duck spotted them and came waddling through the reeds. The other ducklings followed and they all rushed up to Daisy. Quack, quack, welcome back!

Daisy was almost knocked over—they were so excited. And they all gathered around and made a big fuss and we were watching and Annie cried a little, and I sniffed but I didn't cry. Even Caleb was choked up.

Ella's hands hurt from typing so much, so she stopped. Out of her bedroom window she saw Mrs. Brooks and Miss Elliot come into the yard with Annie. The evening shadows were long. Charlie let out an ear-splitting *EE-AW!*

Something's going on, Ella thought, leaving her diary and rushing down.

"Hey, Ella, Miss Elliot would like to talk to your mom," Annie said. "Is she around?"

"She's in the stables with Dad and Caleb," Ella replied.

"And I wouldn't mind a tiny peek at your little Shetland pony," Mrs. Brooks added. "Annie tells me she's very sweet."

"Of course! Come in." Happily, Ella led the way.

Inside the stables they found Caleb

mucking out Charlie's stall, and Mom and Dad busily working on Rosie's hooves. While Dad worked with a strong pair of clippers, Mom smoothed the hooves with a file. Meanwhile, Rosie stood with her nose in her hay-net, contentedly chewing.

Mom was the first to look up and greet the visitors. "Hello, Linda. Hello, Miss Elliot. What a nice surprise!"

The elderly lady smiled broadly. "I expect you heard about the drama down by the pond?"

"We heard all right!" Dad lowered Rosie's hoof and grinned. "Ella hasn't stopped talking about it!"

"She was incredible!" Miss Elliot insisted. "So were Caleb and Annie. And so are you, Heidi. And Mark, of course."

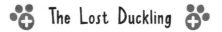

"I agree," Mrs. Brooks added quietly. Then she blushed. "Beautiful little pony," she said, changing the subject.

Ee-aw! Charlie brayed.

"Not forgetting the beautiful donkey," Miss Elliot conceded.

There was silence for a while except for the rasp of Mom's file against Rosie's hoof. Then Miss Elliot slipped

her hand into her jacket pocket and
spoke again.

"I have something for you," she said
shyly, offering Mom a long slip of
paper.

Mom came to the door and took it.
"It's a check!"

Ella glanced at Caleb and Annie, who
shrugged. *Don't ask me!*

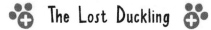

Mom read the numbers. "A check for a very large amount of money," she gasped. "Made out to Animal Magic!"

"For you and your wonderful rescue center!" Miss Elliot insisted. "And for all the good work you do."

Dad came over and stared at the check over Mom's shoulder. He shook his head in astonishment. "This means we can pay our overdue bills and continue on without worrying about money for a long time," he said.

Ella, Caleb, and Annie stared at Miss Elliot.

"Are you sure about this?" Mom asked, holding out the check as if offering it back.

Of course she's sure! Ella thought, quick as a flash.

Miss Elliot pushed the check away again. "Since I sold my house, I have more money than I'll ever need for myself," she insisted. "It would please me beyond words to make this donation."

"Take it!" Mrs. Brooks urged.

And so it was agreed. Animal Magic Rescue Center could continue matching the perfect pet with the perfect owner!

"I feel another celebration coming on!" Dad exclaimed. "A giant pizza and chocolate cake all around!"

EE-AW! Charlie said.

Rosie gave Dad a little don't-forget-me shove from behind and everyone laughed.

"Beautiful little thing!" Mrs. Brooks whispered, offering Rosie a mint from her pocket. "I wonder," she said softly with a faraway look in her eye. "I wonder if

there's room in my field for one adorable
Shetland pony...."